Chamelia
and the New Kid in Class

D1245170

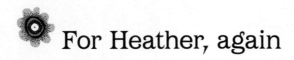 **For Heather, again**

About this book

The illustrations for this book were created with digital collage, using original photos and textures arranged in Adobe Photoshop. Chamelia's and Cooper's outfits were inspired by fabrics generously provided by Alexander Henry Fabrics, Inc. (www.ahfabrics.com), and the cupcake images were used with permission of Blue Bird Bake Shop in Orlando, Florida (www.bluebirdbakeshop.com).

This book was edited by Connie Hsu and designed by Liz Casal
under the art direction of Patti Ann Harris. The production was supervised
by Charlotte Veaney, and the production editor was Christine Ma.
The text and display type are set in Barcelona.

No part of this publication may be reproduced, stored in a retrieval system, or transmitted in any form or by any means, electronic, mechanical, photocopying, recording, or otherwise, without written permission of the publisher. For information regarding permission, write to Little, Brown Books for Young Readers, a division of Hachette Book Group, Inc., 1290 Avenue of the Americas, New York, NY 10104.

ISBN 978-0-545-92537-2

Copyright © 2013 by Ethan Long. All rights reserved. Published by Scholastic Inc., 557 Broadway, New York, NY 10012, by arrangement with Little, Brown Books for Young Readers, a division of Hachette Book Group, Inc. SCHOLASTIC and associated logos are trademarks and/or registered trademarks of Scholastic Inc.

12 11 10 9 8 7 6 5 4 3 2 1   15 16 17 18 19 20/0

Printed in the U.S.A.   40

First Scholastic printing, September 2015

Chamelia

and the New Kid in Class

by Ethan Long

SCHOLASTIC INC.

It was the first day of school, and Chamelia's friends were excited to hear about her summer vacation. Naturally, she chose to tell them through song and dance.

Suddenly, her audience stopped watching.
"Children," said Mrs. Knight, "this is Cooper, your new classmate."
Everyone gathered around Cooper—everyone except for
Chamelia, who was just finishing Act One.

HI!

Cooper made friends fast.

In art class, all the kids wanted *him* to draw their portraits.

For the first time, no one paid any attention to *Chamelia's* works of art.

COOL!

During recess, Cooper won the game—and even more friends.

Chamelia was *not* used to losing.

After school, Cooper's new games were a hit,
but Chamelia didn't think they were special at all.

Besides, she had better things to do.

Cooper kept showing up wherever Chamelia went . . . even the supermarket!
He was seriously getting on her nerves.

When Cooper brought frosted cupcakes to school for his birthday,
Chamelia was not impressed.

She bet they didn't even taste that good.

When Show-and-Tell Day came, it was time
to show everyone who the *real* star was.
Chamelia knew she had to be the best.

So Chamelia pulled out all the stops.

She danced.   She juggled.

She was a star!

Then it was Cooper's turn.
Even though Chamelia's shell collection was a hit,
Cooper's rocks looked really good, too.

He had to be stopped.

So she did all she could to distract him. She yawned.

She blew raspberries.

Her plan was working!

But as she watched Cooper, Chamelia got a heavy, horrible feeling in her stomach.

Suddenly, being the best felt the worst.

So she decided to change her game plan and show the class
what it really meant to be a star.

As it turned out, Cooper's rock collection *was* really good.
So Chamelia cheered.

She applauded.

She was his biggest fan!

Chamelia could finally admit that the new kid was a star, too.

In fact, Cooper was supersweet!

That was all the more reason to make him a best friend...

...and an excellent sidekick!